THE USBORNE YOUNG SCIENTIST
COMPUTERS

Brian Reffin-Smith and Lisa Watts

Edited by Lynn Inglis

Designed by Robert Walster, Graham Round and Iain Ashman

Illustrated by Sean Wilkinson, Peter Bull, Chris Harker and Robert Walster

D1370100

Contents

Technical consultant: Mandy Ingleby

What is a computer?

Put very simply, a computer is a machine which "does things to information". In more scientific terms, it is an "information processor". A computer is given information (called "data") and a set of instructions (called a "program") telling it what to do with the information. It then shows us the results. The data put into the computer is called the "input", and the results which come out are known as the "output".

Since computers were first developed in the 1950s, they have become an ever more important part of everyday life. You are likely to come across them almost anywhere you go and whatever you do. Even this book was produced using computers.

What computers are good at

Here are some of the advantages that computers have over people.

Speed: computers are super-fast. They can process data thousands of times faster than humans.

Quantity: computers are best at working with vast amounts of data. People can only deal with small amounts of information.

Multi-tasking: computers can do many different things at once, whereas people are best at concentrating on one thing at a time.

Memory: computers store lots of data in a small space and can find things almost instantly in their memories. People need time to find information, and then forget much of it.

Precision: computers are accurate because they store their instructions and data. Humans often forget things or make mistakes.

Predictability: computers always perform a task in exactly the same way, as they are programmed. Humans may follow a routine but never do things just the same every time.

Reliability: unlike humans, computers never get hungry, tired, bored or change their minds. They never decide to switch off for a rest or go away on holiday, but they do wear out and get replaced by better models.

But remember! Humans invented and program computers. We possess many qualities that computers do not, such as flexibility, adaptability, creativity and perceptiveness. People may make mistakes, but they can spot them and change their behaviour quickly without having to be re-programmed or have new parts bolted on.

Old and new computers

This picture shows a small, modern computer, the sort used in many millions of offices and homes all over the world. It is running a graphics program and has been used to produce a picture of Stonehenge.

Some people say that Stonehenge itself was a kind of computer. Prehistoric people used it to work out their calendar from the position of the shadows made by the Sun shining on the stones. If you think of the stones as the computer, the sunlight is the input and the calendar is the output.

The programs that instruct the computer are stored on thin, flexible, magnetic disks. Computers can run many different programs and be used to do different things at different times. Next time it is used, this computer could run a word processor instead of a graphics program.

New information is typed in at the keyboard, which has letters and numbers like an ordinary typewriter, but it also has special instruction keys. These keys perform different functions, depending upon what the computer has been programmed to do.

The results of the computer's calculations are shown as a picture on the screen. The picture could also be printed out as "hard copy" on a colour printer.

Special function keys

Input and output

The computer below uses disks and keyboard for input and the screen for output, but there are many ways of getting information in and out of a computer. Here are some examples of other input and output devices.

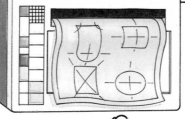

Plotter - output

Pictures and words can be drawn on a "plotter". Signals from the computer guide the pen across the paper. Most plotters can automatically pick up a pen of a new colour.

Graphics tablet - input

Information, such as drawings and graphs, can be put into a computer by drawing on the sensitive surface of a graphics pad or tablet.

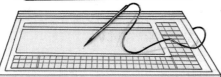

Printer - output

Some printers only print letters and figures, others print graphics, too, and some work in colour. Printers have to be fast to keep up with the flow of information from a computer.

Bar codes - input

Look out for bar codes like this on packages in stores. Details about the product are given to a computer by scanning the lines and spaces with a low-power laser beam.

Music keyboard - input

Computers can also manipulate sounds. This musical keyboard can be programmed to sound like any kind of instrument. It can even use other noises which you record yourself.

Scanner - input

A scanner works like a photocopier, but sends the image into the computer, instead of making a copy. The picture is shown on the screen and can be altered and used.

Mouse - input

As you move a mouse around on your desk, it sends signals to the computer to move a pointer around the screen. You use this to point at and choose on-screen instructions. Clicking one of the buttons on the mouse tells the computer to carry out the instruction being pointed at.

The mouse glides on a ball-bearing inside the case.

Icons - input

The on-screen instructions which the mouse pointer uses are often pictures, known as icons. These represent the instruction to the computer. With a graphics program, for example, by choosing the pencil icon you make the computer draw lines. Choosing the spray-can icon produces an airbrush effect, choosing the brush icon fills in an area with colour.

On-screen menu of icons

Pointer moved by the mouse.

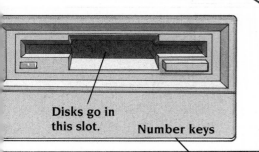

Disks go in this slot.

Number keys

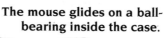

Types of computer

Once, all computers were very big, very expensive, used a lot of power and had to be kept in a specially air-conditioned and cooled room. Today you can slip a computer into your pocket. Over the fifty years since the first computers were developed, computers have become ever smaller, more powerful and more common. The small home or office computers of today are equivalent in power and speed to the largest and most expensive computers of the 1960s. This page shows some kinds of computers and the things that they are used for.

Mainframes

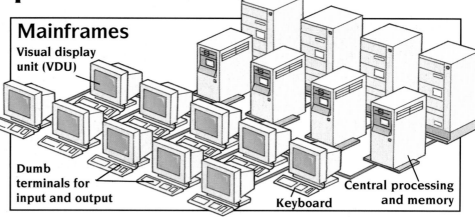

Visual display unit (VDU)

Dumb terminals for input and output

Keyboard

Central processing and memory

Mainframes are large, powerful computers - so big they may fill several rooms and so fast they can do many things at once. They are used to do jobs that involve storing and processing huge volumes of data, such as preparing tax bills and monitoring industrial processes. A mainframe has many "dumb terminals" - keyboards and screens without their own processing and memory - and all users are linked to a central computer.

Minicomputers

Central processing

Printer

Dumb terminals

A minicomputer is smaller than a mainframe, but still far too large to sit on a desk. It cannot handle so much data or work as fast as a mainframe, but is still very powerful and used for similar jobs. Minis are generally used for one particular job, whereas a mainframe does lots of different things, often all at the same time.

Microcomputers

Processing and memory inside here.

Screen

When smaller, cheaper microcomputers, like this, were developed, many more people could afford a computer. They are often called personal computers (PCs), and although not as powerful as mainframes or minis, they can run all kinds of programs and can be used with different input and output equipment.

Computer networks

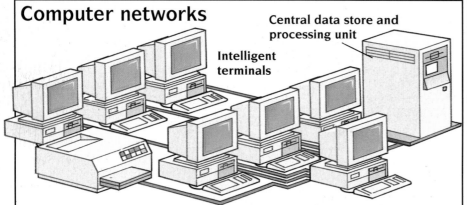

Central data store and processing unit

Intelligent terminals

Here all the users have their own "intelligent terminals" with on-board memory and processing power, like an ordinary microcomputer. The terminals are also linked together and to additional central memory and processing units. This is known as "networking". It allows all the computers to communicate and to share some data and software. This is useful for data which needs to be updated often and used by everyone.

Laptop computer

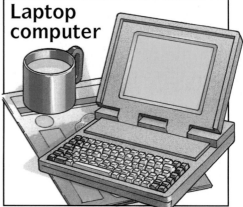

This is a portable micro with built-in screen, data storage and power supply. It runs the same range of programs as the micro and can be connected to a printer, full-size screen or another computer.

Parts of a computer

This picture shows the main parts of a computer, where all the work is done. Every computer has these basic parts, though a mainframe, for instance, may have a bigger memory and a more powerful central processing unit than a smaller microcomputer.

Central processing unit, or CPU

This is the control centre of the computer. All the instructions and information entering the computer come here first and are sent to the correct part of the computer for processing. When the work is finished, the CPU collects the results and sends them to the output.

Power supply

All computers use electricity. Most plug into the mains*, but portable computers may use batteries.

Clock

A quartz crystal "clock" pulsing millions of times each second, controls the speed of the computer.

Memory

Instructions, data and results are stored here by the CPU until they are needed. There is also a permanent store of instructions which tells the computer how to operate.

Input

Input is the flow of information into the computer from the keyboard or other input equipment.

Arithmetic unit

This is where the computer does all its calculations, and sorts and compares data.

*Electrical outlets (US)

Output

Output is the flow of results from the computer to the output equipment.

You can find out how all these parts work, and many other things about computers, on the next few pages.

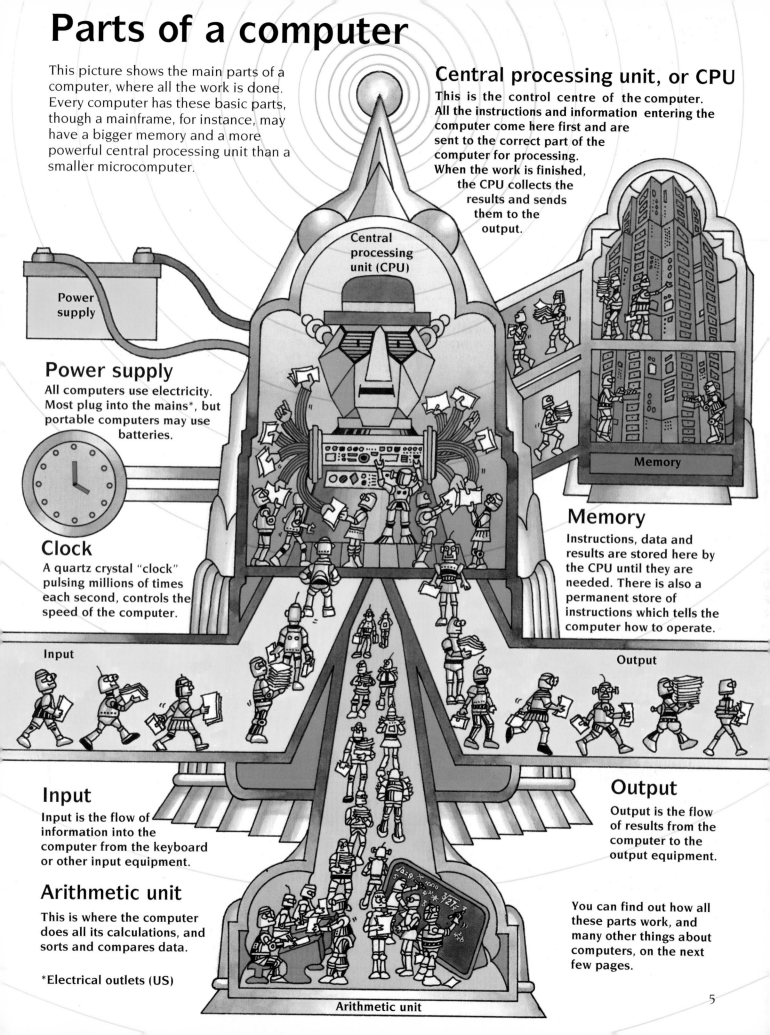

Power supply

Central processing unit (CPU)

Memory

Input

Output

Arithmetic unit

Inside a computer

Pulses of electricity do all the work inside computers, controlled by parts called electronic components. The components in the first computers were called valves. In the 1950s, a new kind of component, called the transistor, was invented.

With transistors it was possible to build much smaller, faster and more reliable computers. The greatest advance, though, came with the development of the integrated circuit, or "chip", in the 1960s. A chip is a tiny slice of a substance called silicon, on which millions of components are packed closely together.

Valves. transistors and chips

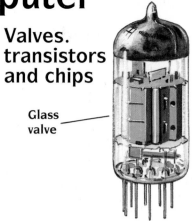

Glass valve

Transistor

Plastic case containing silicon chip.

Glass valves, like the one shown above, were large, used a lot of power, got very hot and were unreliable. The smaller, cheaper transistors could be packed closer together, used much less power and therefore were cooler.

Integrated circuits (chips) are tiny, but contain the equivalent of millions of transistors, all linked together to form a circuit through which electricity can flow.

1 How chips are made

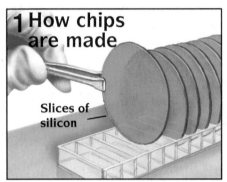

Slices of silicon

To make the chips, crystals of silicon 99.9999999% pure are grown in a vacuum oven. The silicon is so pure that it will not conduct electricity until treated with certain chemicals. The silicon is sliced into thin "wafers" and up to 500 chips will be made from each wafer.

2 Circuit design

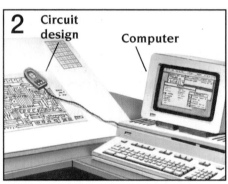

Computer

Some chips have eleven or more different circuits, each containing tens of thousands of components. They are built up, one on top of the other, in the silicon. The circuits are designed using a computer and drawn up 250 times larger than they will be on the finished chip.

3

The circuit designs are then reduced to chip size and photographically printed on the silicon wafer, one at a time. A circuit will not work if even a tiny speck of dust gets on it, so all work is done in an ultra-clean, air-conditioned room, and workers wear sterile suits and masks.

4

The silicon wafers are placed in a furnace at a temperature of over 1,000 °C (1,830 °F) and exposed to certain chemical elements. In the great heat of the furnace, atoms of the chemicals enter the surface of the silicon, but only along the printed lines of the circuits.

5

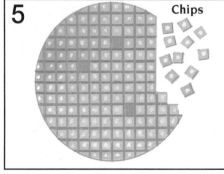

Chips

Stages three and four are repeated until all of the circuits are chemically etched on the chip, on top of each other. The chips are then each tested to see if an electric current can pass through the circuits. The wafer is cut into individual chips by a diamond or laser saw.

6

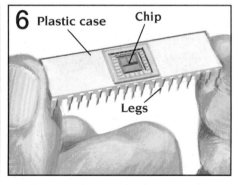

Plastic case

Chip

Legs

Chips have to be perfect - many are faulty and thrown away. Each tiny chip is put into a plastic case with gold wires connecting the circuits to the pins on the case. This is done to make the chip easier to handle and to put into the equipment it will become part of.

Some silicon chips (without their plastic cases) are so tiny they can fit through the eye of a needle. Yet each chip contains more electronic components than the room-sized computers of 40 years ago. On this enlarged chip, the lines are the circuits which contain the components and through which the electric current passes.

Kinds of chips

CPU chip

Microprocessor chip

Memory chip

There are lots of different kinds of chips and each is designed to do a certain job. There are special chips for the central processing unit of the computer and for the memory store, and others to do the work in the arithmetic unit. Some chips can do the work of all the different parts of a computer. These are called microprocessors.

Computer on a chip

This is an enlarged picture of the circuits on a microprocessor chip, showing the parts which do the same work as a computer. Chips like this are used in computers, as well as calculators, electronic games, and equipment such as washing machines.

—Actual size of chip.   Enlarged view of chip.

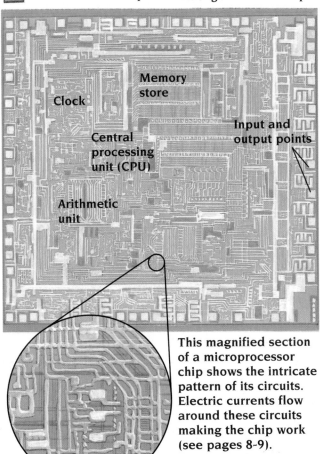

Memory store

Clock

Input and output points

Central processing unit (CPU)

Arithmetic unit

This magnified section of a microprocessor chip shows the intricate pattern of its circuits. Electric currents flow around these circuits making the chip work (see pages 8-9).

Building a computer

The chips for each part of the computer are mounted on boards called printed circuit boards. The chips are connected together by narrow bands of metal printed on the board, which carry the electricity to the chips. The boards are put together to make the computer.

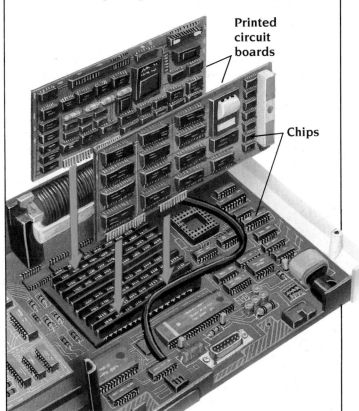

Printed circuit boards

Chips

This picture shows the inside of a small computer. You can see how little space the chips and circuit boards need. Silicon chips, which are very cheap to produce, have made it possible to build very small, powerful computers like this, more cheaply than even before.

How computers work

How can a computer which contains only a mass of silicon chips, process a number, a word or even a picture? The answer is that the electric current which passes through the chips does so in a series of pulses. These form a code which can represent anything at all - numbers, letters or even colours.

The code of pulses is created by the transistors in the chips. These act like switches, turning the current on and off. While the computer is working, millions of pulses are passing through the circuits of the chips every second.

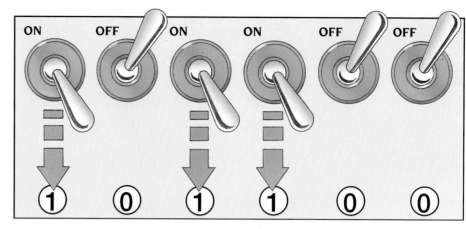

Computers use a very simple code, consisting of only two signals: pulse and no-pulse, or "on" and "off". This is called binary code.

Another way of expressing it, which makes it easier to write down, is with the digits "1" for pulse and "0" for no-pulse, as shown above.

Counting in binary code

The numbers we normally use are called decimal numbers, but you could write numbers in binary code instead. The pictures below show how.

In the decimal system there are ten digits and the system is based on tens. Each of the digits in a number is ten times the value of the digit on its right. For instance, the number 1,463 means, reading from the right-hand side:

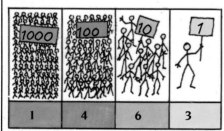

1	4	6	3

3 lots of 1	=	3
6 lots of 10	=	60
4 lots of 100	=	400
1 lot of 1000	=	1000
which added together	=	1463

or one thousand, four hundred and sixty-three.

In the binary system there are two digits and the system is based on twos. Each of the digits in a number is twice the value of the digit on its right. For instance, the binary number 1101 means, reading from right to left:

1	1	0	1

1 lot of 1	=	1
0 lot of 2	=	0
1 lot of 4	=	4
1 lot of 8	=	8
which added together	=	13

So 1101 in binary is thirteen in our number system.

Finger computer

Here is an easy way to change binary numbers into decimal.

Hold up your right hand with the palm towards you. Use a pen to write "1" on your first finger, "2" on the second finger, "4" on the third and "8" on the fourth finger.

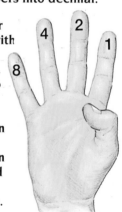

To use your finger computer, stick fingers up for the binary "1s" and fold them down for binary "0s". Then add the numbers on the fingers sticking up and the total is the answer in decimal numbers.

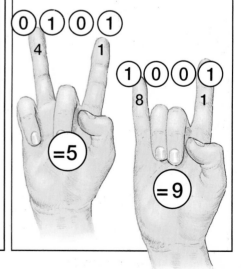

How computers use the code

The stream of pulses travelling through the circuits is controlled by the transistors switching on and off, sending pulses on round the circuit, or holding them back. These transistor switches are also called gates, and there are lots of different kinds. A simple gate has only two points, called terminals, where it receives pulses. Whether or not it sends on a pulse depends on the pulses it receives.

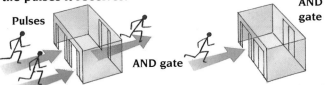

One kind of gate sends on a pulse only when it receives a pulse at both terminals. This is called an AND gate.

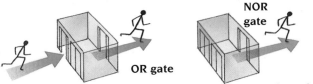

Another kind, called an OR gate, sends on a pulse when it receives a pulse at one or both terminals. A NOR gate only sends one on if neither terminal receives a pulse.

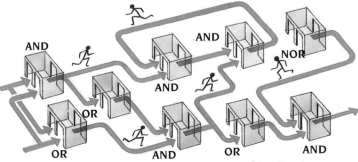

Thousands of these gates are arranged in circuits to create patterns of pulses which can add, compare, memorize and do all the other work inside a computer.

Computerized space pictures

With a code of hundreds of thousands of pulses, the computer can deal with almost anything. For example, given a fuzzy, indistinct picture of a planet taken from a space probe, the computer can help scientists to work out details in the picture.

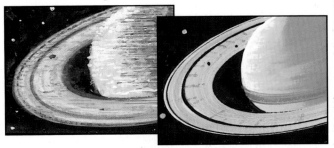

The computer is given a black and white picture like the one on the left and told to analyze all the different shades in it. Then it is instructed to make all the areas of the picture in "shade one" red, all the areas in "shade two" orange, and so on.

By repeating this process lots of times, the computer can make a picture, like the one on the right, which shows the planet more clearly. The colours are used to make the shape clearer and are not the actual colours of the planet.

How to write messages in binary code

Draw six lines.

| A B C D E F G H I J K L M N O P Q R S T U V W X Y Z | 0 1 2 3 4 5 6 7 8 9 |

This diagram shows how a pattern of pulses (dark dashes) can represent letters and numbers, say, on a piece of magnetic tape. Each letter and number is shown by a vertical column of pulses and no-pulses. The pulses are binary "1s" and the no-pulses are "0s".

To write messages in this code, draw lines across a piece of paper, as shown. Then for each letter in the message, make dashes between the correct lines as shown in the guide on the left. Leave spaces between each word. Can you work out the word shown above?*

*The answer is on page 32.

9

The computer's memory

In the electronic circuits of its memory, the computer holds a vital store of instructions, data and results. This ability to store information enables it to carry out very difficult calculations by working through them step-by-step, storing the results of each stage and checking and comparing them with later results and information.

Data and programs can be stored on magnetic disks and tapes. These are used as back-up memory, for transferring information between computers and as permanent storage of data and software.

Bits — Byte

Computerized information is stored in binary code. The binary digits "1" and "0" are also called "bits". To record all the letters of the alphabet, as well as numbers and signs, the computer needs more than the four combinations: 10, 01, 11, 00, which are possible with the two bits. So each letter or number is usually represented by a group of eight bits, called a "byte".

A computer's memory is measured by the number of bytes it can store. This is expressed in "kilobytes" or "K" (1,024 bytes), or "megabytes" or "Mb" (over 1,000,000 bytes).

Built-in memory

ROM

RAM

Inside the computer there are two types of memory. One, called ROM, is a permanent store of instructions telling the computer how to work. The letters stand for Read Only Memory. The computer can only read the information in ROM, and you cannot rub it out or put new information there. The instructions in ROM are built into the computer when it is made.

The other type of memory is called RAM, which stands for Random Access Memory. This is where the computer stores all the data and instructions it receives from the input, and the results as it works through its calculations. RAM is a short-term memory - when the computer is switched off all the information disappears. The ROM, however, is long-term memory and stays intact.

Human memory

Like computers, people also have a permanent, or long-term memory, and a short-term memory (called LTM and STM for short). Here is a memory test to try out on a friend.

On two large pieces of paper write out the letters as shown below.

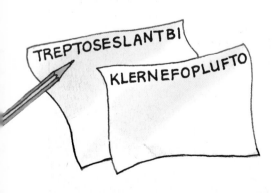

TREPTOSESLANTBI
KLERNEFOPLUFTO

Say to your friend: "I am going to show you some letters for a few seconds. Wait until I give you the signal, then write down what you remember." Hold up one set of the letters for about five seconds. Cover them up, wait ten seconds then signal by tapping something.

Now repeat the test with the other letters. This time, instead of giving a signal, say: "OK, you can write them down now." The person probably gets fewer right this time, as your spoken instruction has to be stored in STM too, and pushes out some of the letters.

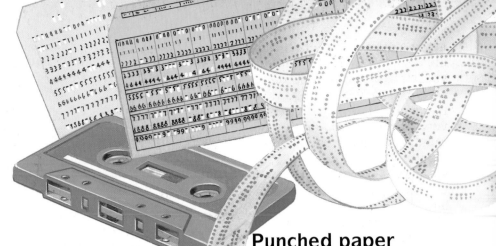

Memory store outside the computer

Once it is switched off, the computer forgets what is in its RAM and so all the information in this memory is lost. To save this information permanently you need a back-up store.

The earliest computers used punched cards or paper tape for this. The information is stored as patterns of holes which the computer can "read", with a hole representing binary "1" and no hole representing binary "0".

Next came magnetic tape, where the binary code is stored as electrical charges on the tape. Although tapes are still used, most computers today use magnetic disks.

Magnetic tape

Large mainframes use huge reels of magnetic tape for data storage and small home micros can use ordinary cassette tapes. Tapes are delicate but can be re-used.

Punched paper cards and tape

These are flimsy, prone to break down in use and difficult to store. They also hold much less information than magnetic storage and cannot be re-used.

Disks

Disks are much faster to use than tapes as the computer can read information from anywhere on the disk, instantly. This is known as "random access". A tape, on the other hand, has to be run from the beginning each time.

Like tape, disks store data magnetically. The electrical on/off signals produced by the computer are turned into magnetic signals by a read/write head in the disk drive. The disk spins beneath the read/write head and these magnetic signals are recorded on its magnetically sensitive surface. The read/write head can then read them again later.

CD-ROM

CD-ROM stands for "Compact Disk-Read Only Memory" and these are shiny, plastic disks like music CDs. The binary code is stored as microscopic pits on the disk surface, which can be "read" by a tiny laser beam. Unlike floppy and hard disks, CD-ROMs cannot be wiped and re-recorded.

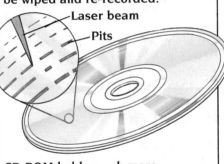

Laser beam
Pits

CD-ROM holds much more information than floppy or hard disks. One small disk can hold eighty million words (twice as many as the whole of the *Encyclopedia Britannica*). CD-ROM can also be used to store moving video images, which take up too much memory for floppy disks.

CD-ROM

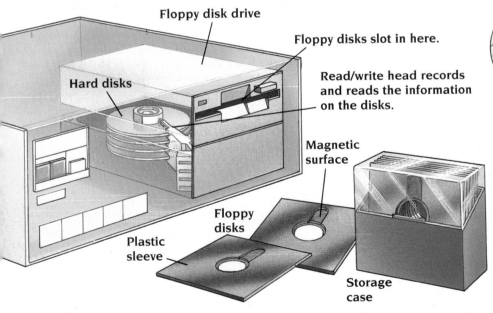

Floppy disk drive

Floppy disks slot in here.

Read/write head records and reads the information on the disks.

Hard disks

Magnetic surface

Floppy disks

Plastic sleeve

Storage case

There are two types of disks: floppy and hard. Floppy disks are thin, flexible circles of plastic, coated with magnetic material, with a protective outer sleeve. They are put into the disk drive when the data or programs they hold are needed.

Hard disks are similar circles of magnetically surfaced plastic, but are built into the computer as a permanent part of the machine. They hold more information than floppies and work faster too, rather like using 40 floppy disks at once.

11

Telling the computer what to do

A computer program is a list of instructions telling the computer what to do.* Some programs, known as system software, control the essential operations of the computer, and these are stored permanently on ROMs built into the computer.

Other programs, called application software, tell it exactly what to do for a specific job, such as word processing. These are usually stored on disk to be loaded into the computer when needed.

All programs must be carefully written as errors will lead to mistakes in the computer's work.

1 Stupid peanut program

NO PEANUTS

1. LEAVE HOME
2 GO TO SHOP, ASK FOR PEANUTS
3 IF SHOP HAS NONE, GO BACK TO LINE 2
4 GO HOME

Here is a list of instructions for buying peanuts, written as if it is a program for a computer. There are some mistakes in this program, though. Can you spot them? Mistakes in a program are called "bugs" and mean that the computer cannot carry out its job properly.

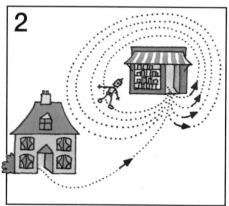

There are two bugs in the peanut program. Line 2 does not tell the computer to try a new shop, so it would keep going to the same shop and asking for peanuts.

The other bug is in line 3. It does not tell the computer when to stop, so even if there were no peanuts anywhere, the computer would go on trying to find some.

1 LEAVE HOME
2 GO TO NEAREST SHOP NOT ALREADY VISITED. ASK FOR PEANUTS.
3 IF SHOP HAS NONE GO TO LINE 2. DO THIS ONLY TEN TIMES.
4 GO HOME.

This is a better version as it tells the computer to go home once it has peanuts, to visit different shops if the previous one has none, and puts a limit of ten shops into the program.

Flowcharts

The most important stage in solving a problem like this with a computer is studying the problem very carefully. You have to work out what information the computer needs and what steps it should go through, before starting to write the program.

One way of doing this is to draw a flowchart, showing the sequence of steps in the program. A computer can act on only one piece of information at a time, so you have to work out the steps very precisely and make sure that they are in the right order.

The finished program is written in chunks, by choosing the right computer code for each instruction, at every step.

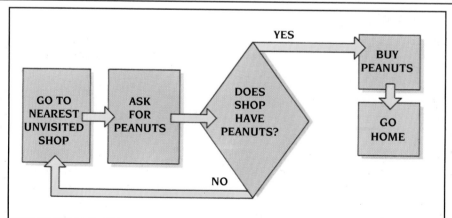

GO TO NEAREST UNVISITED SHOP → ASK FOR PEANUTS → DOES SHOP HAVE PEANUTS? — YES → BUY PEANUTS → GO HOME — NO

This is part of a flowchart for the peanut-buying program. Flowcharts are always drawn with boxes of different shapes for the different steps in the program. Instructions to the computer are in rectangular boxes, questions about the problem are in diamond-shaped boxes. Try making a flowchart for getting ready for school in the morning.

*Never "programme" in computer jargon.

Programming languages

Once you have decided what you want the computer to do and worked out a flowchart to analyze the problem, you are ready to write a program to make the computer do it. You have to translate the contents of each box on the flowchart into a simple programming language.

Computers actually all "speak" the same language - binary code. It is possible to program the computer directly in this code but it would be extremely difficult to do. It is much easier to use a special programming language. There are many different programming languages, each developed to suit different sorts of problems.

```
400 PRINT "ENTER CO-ORDINATES"
410 N=0
420 INPUT X(N), Y(N)
430 IF X(N)=0 AND Y(N)=0
440 N=N+1:GOTO 420
450 FOR I=1 TO N
460 X(I)=X(I)+100
470 NEXT I
480 PRINT"ENTER ROTATION
490 INPUT RX,RY,RZ
500 PRINT"PLOTTER <P>
510 INPUT Z$
```

This is part of a program written in a language called BASIC, telling the computer to draw the picture on the right. Each of the instructions in a program is numbered and the

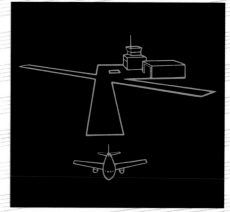

computer works logically through them. The lines are numbered in tens, so that extra lines of code can be added later, in between, without having to renumber every line.

BASIC runs on microcomputers and is often used to teach people about computers and programming. It is easy to use and learn as many of the terms are based on familiar English words and mathematical symbols.

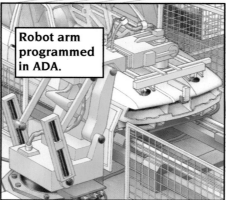

Robot arm programmed in ADA.

Languages designed to run on mainframes and minicomputers include COBOL for business software, Pascal for controlling processes in factories, FORTRAN for mathematics and ADA for robotics.

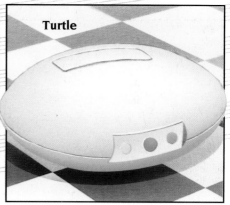

Turtle

Professor Seymour Papert developed a language called LOGO for children to learn. It is used to draw pictures by controlling a robot turtle which crawls round the floor with a pen, leaving a trail.

Language levels

The programming languages mentioned above, like BASIC and COBOL, are all examples of "high-level" computer languages. These are so called because they are relatively easy for people to understand and use.

However, for the computer to understand these high-level languages they must first be translated into binary code. This is done by special programs used by the computer, called the compiler and assembler. These programs plus others which make the different parts of the computer, such as the screen and keyboard, all work together are known as the operating system.

Different makes of computer have different operating systems, which is why programs written for one type of computer will not run on another type.

There are also "low-level" languages, such as assembly language, which are closer to binary code and so quicker and easier for the computer to understand. These languages are much more difficult for human programmers to write in, but produce programs which run more efficiently and faster than those written in a high-level language.

However, most people do not write their own programs but buy them ready made.

Application software

This is the name given to the programs which you buy to make your computer do the jobs you want. Computers can be programmed to do almost anything. The average personal computer could be used for word processing, financial calculations, producing graphics, playing games, or storing and sorting data, for example.

There are many software manufacturers and so you have a big choice of application software packages.

Mainframe and minicomputers often have their programs specially written for the job they have to do, rather than using "off the shelf" commercial programs.

13

Funny poem program

These two pages show you how to make a cardboard "computer" which can write 16,384 different poems.

You will need a strip of paper 60cm x 6cm (24in x 2in) - if necessary, tape several pieces together to make a strip this long. Also a piece of thin cardboard 12cm x 20cm (5in x 8in), more paper to write on and a pencil, eraser and scissors. You will also need another small piece of cardboard and a used matchstick.

Follow the instructions on this page to make the computer. The next page shows you how to make it write funny poems.

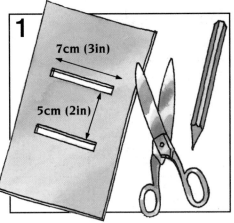

1

Carefully cut two slits in the piece of thin cardboard, as shown above. The slits should be about 5cm (2in) apart and should measure about 7cm (3in) across.

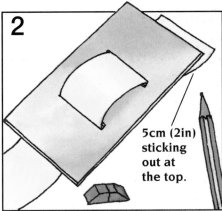

2

Thread the strip of paper through the slits like this. Pull it down so that 5cm (2in) sticks out the back at the top. If it does not slide easily, make the slits wider.

3

Now you are ready to write the program instructions on the strip of paper. First, write instruction one, as shown above, on the paper showing between the slits.

4

Pull the paper up so instruction one disappears, and write instruction two, given above. Leave only about 2cm (1in) space between the instructions.

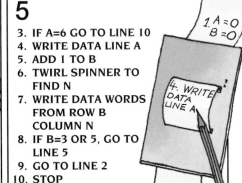

5

3. IF A=6 GO TO LINE 10
4. WRITE DATA LINE A
5. ADD 1 TO B
6. TWIRL SPINNER TO FIND N
7. WRITE DATA WORDS FROM ROW B COLUMN N
8. IF B=3 OR 5, GO TO LINE 5
9. GO TO LINE 2
10. STOP

Continue pulling the paper up and writing all the instructions given above, on the paper strip. Now go on to the section below to find out how the program works.

How it works

The letters A, B and N represent numbers. These numbers show you which data lines and words to use from the lists at the top of the opposite page, to make up the poem.

At the start of the program A and B are at zero, but as you work through the program, the instructions tell you to add one to them, so the numbers change. To remember the values of A, B and N, draw a "memory store" chart, like the one shown here. Pencil in the numbers and erase and change them as you go.

You also need to make a spinner to generate the number for N. Write the numbers one to four on a small square of cardboard and poke a used matchstick through the middle.

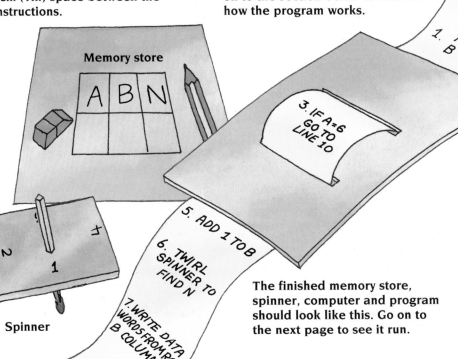

The finished memory store, spinner, computer and program should look like this. Go on to the next page to see it run.

Data lines

These are the "data lines" for the poem. When the program tells you to "Write data line A" find the value of A from the memory store, then write out the data line of the same number.

1. THERE WAS A YOUNG MAN FROM
2. WHO
3. HIS
4. ONE NIGHT AFTER DARK
5. AND HE NEVER WORKED OUT

Data words

These are the data words to complete each line of the poem. Each row contains words suitable for one of the lines. The words you use are decided by the values of B and N as you work through the program. B gives you the number of the row and N is the number of the column.

	Column 1	Column 2	Column 3	Column 4
1	TASHKENT	TRENT	KENT	GHENT
2	WRAPPED UP	COVERED	PAINTED	FASTENED
3	HEAD	HAND	DOG	FOOT
4	IN A TENT	WITH CEMENT	WITH SOME SCENT	THAT WAS BENT
5	IT RAN OFF	IT GLOWED	IT BLEW UP	IT TURNED BLUE
6	IN THE PARK	LIKE A QUARK	FOR A LARK	WITH A BARK
7	WHERE IT WENT	ITS INTENT	WHY IT WENT	WHAT IT MEANT

Running the program

1 Set the program to line one and, as instructed, write zero in the memory store for A and B. Now work through the program and whenever it tells you to add one to A or to B, change the number in the memory store.

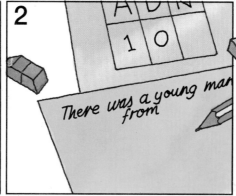

2 When the program tells you to "Write data line A", look in the memory store to find the number for A. Then, from the list above, find the data line with the same number as A. Write it out on a new piece of paper.

3 In line 6, the program tells you to "Twirl spinner to find N". The spinner randomly generates a number, as the side that it leans on when it stops gives you the number for N. Write this in the memory store.

4 When it says "Write data words row B, column N", find the numbers for B and N from the memory store. Then complete the line of the poem with the data words from row number B, column number N.

5 For lines three or eight, if your number for A or B is not the same as the numbers given in the program, miss out that instruction and move on to the next line. This is just how a real program works.

6 Work backwards and forwards through the program until you get to line ten and the poem is finished. If you work through the program again, the "computer" will give a different version of the poem.

Can computers think?

The computers and robots of science fiction can do everything that humans can - and more. Present day computers are not quite so clever, though sometimes their responses do seem almost human, as in the conversation with a computer shown below. This sort of behaviour by a machine is known as artificial intelligence.

The computer's intelligence is not real, though. All computers are entirely controlled by the instructions in their programs. Thinking has to be flexible and creative, things which computers are not capable of, yet.

How computers play chess

Playing chess is often thought to require intelligence, yet computers can do it. Chess is a game played according to unvarying rules. A program for playing chess contains these rules and uses them to work out all the hundreds of possible moves at each stage of the game. It is the speed at which a computer can examine how a move will affect the game, which enables it to play. The best chess computers learn from their mistakes, too. They store all the moves, and their results, from past games and are able to compare these to the present one. At the moment, though, the best human players are still able to beat the best computers.

Conversation with a computer

These pictures illustrate a conversation with a computer. The person types the questions into the keyboard and the computer's answers appear on the screen.

The computer is programmed to recognize certain words, letters and symbols, and to reply to them.

The program also contains a list of ideas and grammar rules which the computer uses to work out its replies.

It also has several standard replies which, although they may appear intelligent, are not specific enough to be very meaningful.

The computer recognizes "O ARE Y" and "?" as a question. This triggers off a standard reply, which fits the question and makes it seem as if the computer understood it.

This time it spots "WHAT IS" and "?" and gives another programmed response to a question. It also spots the word "COMPUTER", but it does not always react to every word in a sentence.

The computer's last reply was unsatisfactory for the human! Here the computer spots "KNOW" and gives its standard reply to that word. But this is yet another unsatisfactory reply.

The computer seems to make an intelligent reply to the first statement, but really has just repeated it and changed one word. It does not recognize "SOMETIMES" and so gives a vague reply.

Machine senses

Before it could think, a computer would need to be able to take in information from the outside world, on its own. It needs senses which mimic the human ones of sight, touch, smell and hearing. These are easy to provide electronically, with video cameras for "vision" and microphones for "hearing".

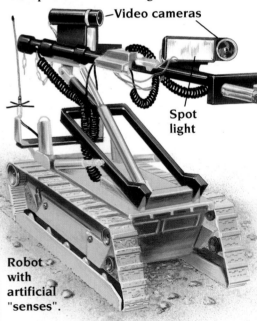

Robot with artificial "senses".

Touch can be simulated by pressure sensitive pads or sensitive wires which work like animal whiskers. "Smell" sensors can be programmed to recognize molecules of particular chemicals by using the appropriate tests. A robot can also have extra senses, such as radar.

Computer recognition

Intelligence depends upon being able to deal with information as well as take it in. You can recognize and understand all the things you see around you, without even thinking about it. This is very difficult for a computer.

For instance, you can recognize all these shapes as the letter "A". Programming a computer to read handwriting is very difficult. It would have to be programmed to recognize all these "A" shapes, and many, many more, plus a similar number for each of the other letters of the alphabet. This has been done, but takes a great deal of processing power and memory.

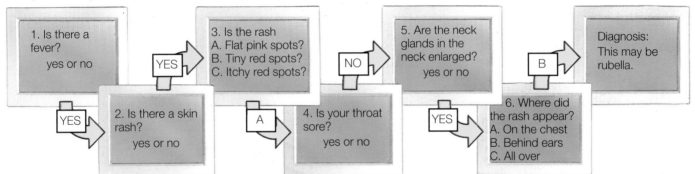

Computers can also learn to recognize faces, but find this equally difficult. Live people are harder for computers to recognize than photographs, as they constantly move around. The computer sees the face from different angles, which it is unable to recognize. Growing a beard or changing a hairstyle will also confuse the computer.

Expert systems

1. Is there a fever?
   yes or no

YES

2. Is there a skin rash?
   yes or no

YES

3. Is the rash
   A. Flat pink spots?
   B. Tiny red spots?
   C. Itchy red spots?

A

4. Is your throat sore?
   yes or no

NO

5. Are the neck glands in the neck enlarged?
   yes or no

YES

6. Where did the rash appear?
   A. On the chest
   B. Behind ears
   C. All over

B

Diagnosis: This may be rubella.

The knowledge of experts can be computerized by creating a program which stores their expertize and allows other people access to it. This kind of software is known as an expert system, and works by the computer asking the user questions to gather the information it needs. For example, a medical expert system, like the one above, may question patients about their symptoms and then provide a diagnosis and treatment for a real doctor to check. Many expert systems have been developed. One helps mechanics mending cars, another helps geologists looking for oil by identifying the most likely combination of rock types, and another helps architects to design buildings. Expert systems are used by experts, rather than untrained people.

Robot truck

Scientists developing undersea and extra-terrestrial robot vehicles, have programmed a computer to drive a van, shown on the right, along a familiar route. It follows a set of rules that tells it how to drive and what to do in all kinds of circumstances, such as turning corners, at road junctions and if people cross the road. The computer operates the steering, brakes and accelerator in response to the road conditions. It uses a video camera to see the road ahead and a laser scanner to read road markings. It is programmed to recognize and avoid certain common "obstacles", like cars, pedestrians and pets, but to ignore others, such as litter.

Things computers can do

The great speed with which computers can work through vast amounts of information makes them good for calculating millions of telephone bills, keeping business records of sales and payments, for scientific calculations and so on. Here, though, are some of the other things that computers can do.

Computers in schools

When they were first introduced into schools, during the 1980s, computers were mainly used by older pupils learning about computer programming or information technology. The computers used in schools and at home were much less powerful than those used in business. Now the same kind of microcomputers are used at work and at school, so children may be using the same computers as their parents.

Computers are used by pupils of all ages and in every subject, from maths and science to art and design. Special software helps pupils to learn about maps and geography, play historical simulation games, and even to compose and play music on an electronic keyboard.

The teaching staff may also use computers to plan timetables, to store student records and to prepare teaching materials.

Model train control

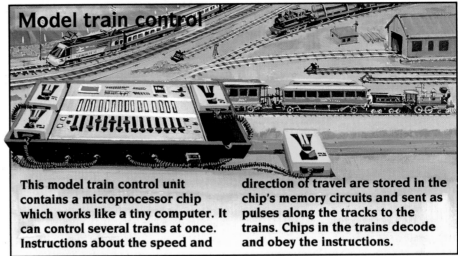

This model train control unit contains a microprocessor chip which works like a tiny computer. It can control several trains at once. Instructions about the speed and direction of travel are stored in the chip's memory circuits and sent as pulses along the tracks to the trains. Chips in the trains decode and obey the instructions.

Medical computers

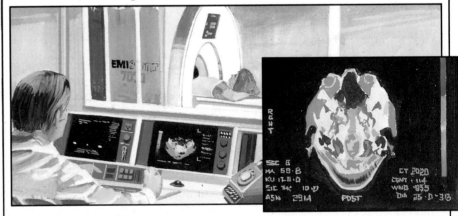

Computerized equipment is used in many areas of medicine, to monitor very ill patients in intensive care, for example. Computers also help doctors diagnose illness. This scanner takes thousands of pictures of the patient from lots of different angles. The computer processes the pictures, displaying them on a screen for the doctors to see.

Digital hairstyles

This computer and video system lets you try out new hairstyles without having your hair cut. Your picture is captured by the video camera and then sent to the computer and displayed on screen. The computer has various hairstyles stored as video images on disk. The hair stylist can then call up these hairstyles and superimpose them in position on the screen image of your head. The computer can make prints of these images for you to take away, like those on the right, showing you with different hairstyles.

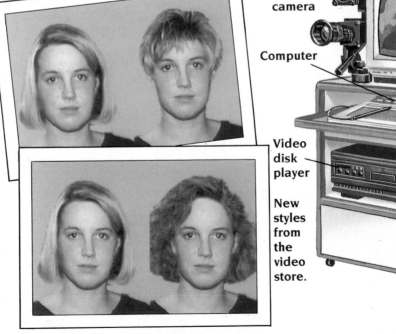

Video camera

Computer

Video disk player

New styles from the video store.

Programmable car

Arrow keys tell the car which way to go.

This toy car is controlled by a microprocessor chip and can be programmed to follow a route. You do this by using the arrow keys inside the car to instruct it to go straight ahead for a certain distance, turn right, turn left and so on.

Language translation

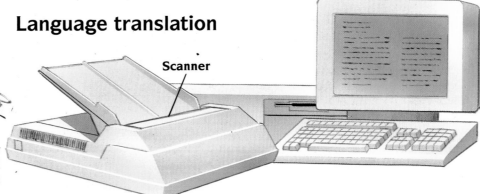

Scanner

It is very difficult for computers to translate from one language to another, as a single word can have different meanings in different sentences. For instance, the computer needs to be given a lot of information before it can recognize the difference between "I feel like a glass of milk" and "I feel like an idiot". Programs which can translate are being developed, though, often using scanning devices to "read" documents directly into the computer's memory.

Logging system

New cars have many coats of paint applied to them. After each one, a supervisor checks the surface under very bright lights to look for specks of dust and other faults. Any found are logged on the electronic pad which has a diagram of the car on the screen. The electronic "pen" is used to touch the diagram in the appropriate place to indicate where and what the fault is.

The pad stores all this information. It can later be connected to another computer which has a program to analyze the faults and spot any recurring problems.

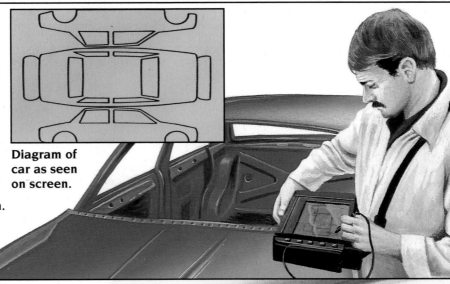

Diagram of car as seen on screen.

Helping disabled people

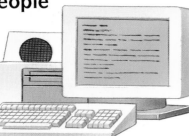

Computers can be a great help to people who have difficulty communicating. This system, for example, has a voice chip which actually speaks the words typed in at the keyboard and shown on the screen. Computer keyboards can also be modified so that disabled people can operate them easily.

Weather forecasting

Computers are used to help meteorologists forecast the weather. Weather satellites in orbit above the Earth and weather stations around the world send in frequent reports of the changes in the winds and temperature which affect the weather.

The computer is used to analyze this mass of data and to produce forecasts. These are continuously updated as the conditions change.

Computers at work

Keeping business records, stock lists, sales accounts, and details of wages and pensions are all common ways that computers can help people working in business and industry.

They can also be used to help managers plan and make decisions, by allowing them to try out different things to see what will happen in various sets of circumstances. Ideas and plans can be tested on the computer before being put into practice. Computers can also help to work out the best way to do complex jobs and even to control the machinery that does the work.

Production monitoring

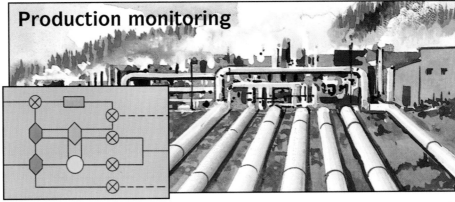

In large automatic production plants, such as power stations, computers can be used to give continual information about all the processes. This allows staff to keep track of what is going on and to watch out for problems. The screen above shows how simple symbols can be used to represent different operations, such as the flow of raw materials and the state of machinery. Production controllers can understand it at a glance.

Decision making

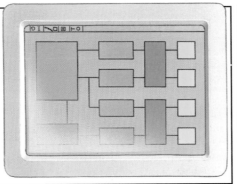

Graphics like this are easier to understand than text.

Deciding what course of action to follow is an important part of business and computers can help managers to do this effectively. Special programs allow planners to test out ideas by asking the computer "what if ?" questions, and comparing the answers. This type of application is similar to the computer simulations shown on page 28.

Problem solving

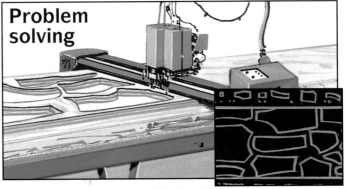

This is a computer-controlled machine for cutting the fabric for clothes. Using a computer, it is much easier for a skilled pattern cutter to work out how to position the pattern pieces so that as little fabric is wasted as possible. The layout of the pieces is stored in the computer's memory and guides the cutting machine.

Robots

Robots controlled by computers can be used instead of people to do repetitive jobs, such as those on a production line in a factory. The robots pictured here are welding the joints on car frames. All their actions are controlled by a program of instructions in the computer. Other, similar robots are used later to spray paint the finished cars.

Some robots are "trained" by people. A worker guides the robot arm through the task and all the movements are stored as a program in the computer's memory. Then, when the program is re-run, the robot repeats the movements exactly. It can be reprogrammed to do another job, but cannot cope with unexpected situations as a human worker could.

Robots and computer-controlled machinery are being used more and more in industry. One advantage of robots is that they can work continuously, so factories can be kept going day and night. Robots can also be used for jobs which are too dangerous for people, such as checking the fuel rods in a nuclear power station.

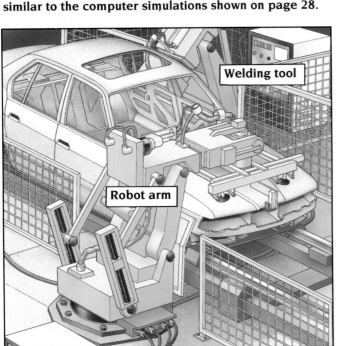

Welding tool

Robot arm

Computers in offices

Computers have revolutionized office work and are used for many different jobs. The four most common kinds of application software used are: spreadsheets, which deal with numbers and calculations; word processors, which deal with text; databases, which manipulate and store information such as addresses, and desktop publishing which is used to create printed material.

Computers help businesses to deal with more information, and to get results faster than is possible by hand. They also allow information to be manipulated in new ways. Below are some ways a phone company could use computers when launching a new service.

Spreadsheets

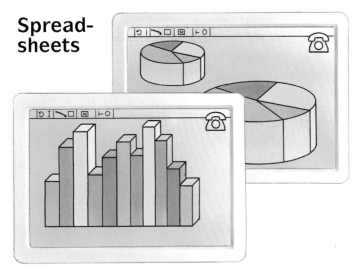

The phone company uses a spreadsheet to try out different charges for its new service, to see which is best. The results are shown as a graph. Spreadsheets perform many different calculations very quickly. The figures can be shown as graphics - graphs or charts - to make them easier to understand. Spreadsheets are also used as "what if?" programs - to help try out different costs and prices, for example, to find the most profitable.

Word processing

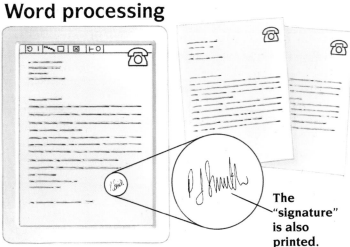

The "signature" is also printed.

Computers are good at typing and printing letters. Mistakes can be changed before they are printed out and some software even checks spelling. A standard letter can be stored on disk to be used many times and personalized by adding each person's name and address, before printing. Even a final signature can be scanned into the computer, stored on disk, and printed at the end of each letter. Here the phone company is preparing letters for customers.

Desktop publishing

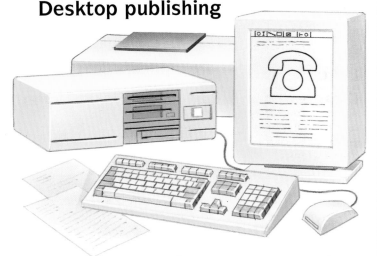

Desktop publishing (DTP) is the production of brochures, leaflets and other printed material on a computer. The software is used to combine text, photographs and other graphics, to make up and print out pages. The computer can be programmed to use different type styles and sizes. Here, the phone company is producing a sales brochure about its new services, to send to customers.

Databases

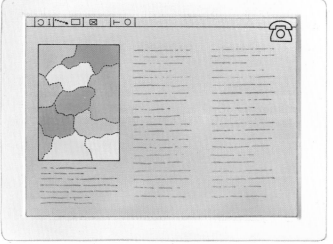

A database is used to store and manipulate information, such as the details of all the customers of a company. It stores information in a specially structured way so that it is easy to find and use in different ways. Here, the phone company is asking the computer for a list of all the people who live in a particular area. They could have chosen to list all customers who have not paid their bills or who have had repairs recently.

Instant information

Information is vitally important in many areas of life. Banks and shops, businesses and factories all rely on computers to process their information, quickly and efficiently. For example, a company might deal with data about clients and their orders, the stock held in store, the wages and tax of staff and the movement of goods. Computers can make handling this kind of information much easier, using software like word-processors and databases, seen on the previous page. These two pages look at some ways in which computers help us to deal with the vast amount of information in our lives today.

Sharing a computer

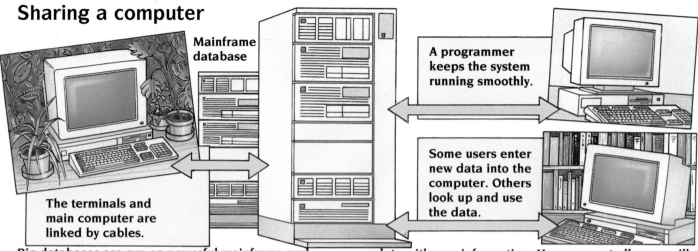

Mainframe database

A programmer keeps the system running smoothly.

Some users enter new data into the computer. Others look up and use the data.

The terminals and main computer are linked by cables.

Big databases are run on powerful mainframe and minicomputers, which can handle millions of pieces of data at once. These work so fast that many people can use them at the same time. When all the users are dealing with the same data (names and addresses and information for making up bills, for example) it is much more efficient to have just one shared database to update with new information. However, not all users will be doing the same things with the data. Some will be typing in new data, others will be looking up data and using it. There may also be programmers making sure that the whole system runs smoothly. The computer actually deals with each person separately. However, it switches from one to another so fast that no one notices a delay.

Computer communications

Computer databases can also be accessed via the telephone system, since phone lines carry conversations as pulses of electricity. Some modern microcomputers can simply be plugged into a telephone socket and call up distant databases. Others need to use a piece of equipment called a modem to make the connection. Special data lines are reserved for computer communications between organizations, such as banks, which are heavy users of computer communications. Data can even be sent internationally between computers, via satellite links.

Satellite

These two distant computers are linked together.

Home "comms"

If you have a home computer you too can communicate with distant databases and other computers over the telephone. (This is often called "comms".)

By using a suitable modem to connect your computer to the telephone system, you can dial up any of the free bulletin boards which advertise in computer magazines. Bulletin boards are small, simple databases that store information and programs. There are also larger, commercial databases, but you have to pay for these and need an identification number and password to get in. Some are of general interest and cover many areas, others cover specialist fields such as medicine.

The phone is connected to a modem, which is connected to the computer.

Telephone

British Rail

Modem   Computer

Virtual reality

Virtual reality computer systems make users feel as if they are actually inside a computer-created environment, that is completely responsive to a user's movements and actions, just like the real world. If you move your head, for example, the visual scene changes. These systems consist of a helmet which contains electronic equipment that picks up movements of the head and sends messages back to a computer. It has two small VDU screens, one for each eye, and speakers over the ears. Some systems also have a glove which gives feedback about hand movements and controls the actions of an on-screen hand. This "flies" through the computer environment and can touch things there.

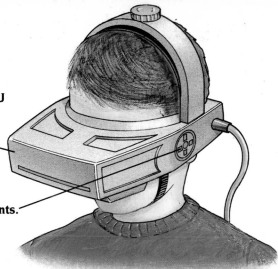

Two small VDU screens go in front of the eyes.

This sensor keeps track of the user's head movements.

A wire connects the helmet to a computer.

CD-ROM

In the past, small microcomputers were not able to hold really big databases as they did not have the storage or processing capacity to deal with so much information. With the development of the CD-ROM, however, it is now possible to store vast quantities of data on a tiny disk. For example, telephone companies sell all the phone numbers in the country stored on CD-ROM.

Some newspapers also produce CD-ROM versions of an entire year's papers. Not only are these easier to store than old newspapers, but the computer can look up every mention of any particular subject.

Computer

CD player

Multi-media

CDs can store moving and still video images and sound, as well as data such as names and text. This marriage of computer and video technologies is known as multi-media, or CD-TV. Using the power of the computer with video means that we have a new way of viewing, using and even interacting with information such as TV programmes.

Video camera

Mouse

Computer security

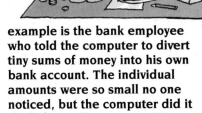

These days, with so much information passing between computers, including orders for goods and electronic payment instructions, a new kind of crime has developed. People, known as hackers, can sometimes intercept computer communications, and even alter the information. To prevent this, computers are programmed only to respond to certain passwords and code numbers, but computer criminals still find ways through. One example is the bank employee who told the computer to divert tiny sums of money into his own bank account. The individual amounts were so small no one noticed, but the computer did it so often it added up to millions.

Computers in everyday life

Computers reach into almost every area of our lives these days, but without us always being aware of it. You may not be able to see the computers involved, or the computer may not look like one with a keyboard and screen. The computer may be tiny and hidden inside a piece of equipment, or huge and a long way away. Here are some examples of places where you may be using computers without realizing it.

At home

This picture shows how many of the things in an ordinary kitchen use microchip computer technology to make them more efficient and easier to use. Many of the services that come into the home also rely upon computers at some stage.

The TV has complex computerized circuits to process the broadcast picture signal. TV stations use computers to help produce and transmit programmes.

Phone and postal companies use computers to help them provide a fast and efficient service (see below).

The freezer has temperature sensors and a microchip programmed to bleep if the door is left open or there is a power cut.

The fridge is programmed to keep the different shelves at different temperatures.

The washer/dryer has a microchip programmed to do different washes and sensors to tell when the laundry is dry.

Phone

The phone system is becoming very computerized, with computer controlled switching to connect you to other numbers. Some systems even carry your voice as computerized, digital signals. You may also be able to program your phone to remember and dial some numbers automatically.

Many offices now have facsimile (fax) machines, which send copies of documents by phone. They work by digitizing the text and pictures into an electronic code that the phone lines can carry.

Post

The post has to be sorted by destination before it can be delivered. When this is done by hand it can be slow. Using computers and individual post- or zip-codes makes it much faster. Each address has its own code of letters and numbers or just numbers. After posting, this code is translated into tiny spots of magnetic ink, which can be "read" by a computer scanner. The computer can tell where each letter is going and sort the post much quicker than humans can.

Many of the official letters will have been written on a word processor, and addressed using a database.

Even the electricity that keeps all this domestic equipment going will have been produced with computer help. Mainframe computers monitor and control the electricity's manufacture and its supply to homes and factories.

Even very ordinary things like shopping and the money that pays for it may be under computer control (see right).

This oven is programmed to cook a meal automatically, turning itself on and off to a pre-set temperature at pre-set times.

Hot water and heating is produced by a programmable boiler with microchip controls and sensors.

Shopping

Many shops use computers for stock and price control. Each product has its own unique bar code. When you buy something this is "read" by a laser scanner at the till. The bar code tells the till what the product is and the price, and these details are printed out on your receipt.

The till records details of everything sold and passes this data on to a main computer. Stock which is running low can then be reordered.

As the information is all on computer it is easy to analyze, to see what is selling well and what is not, for example. Product prices can also be changed automatically, by programming the tills to charge a different price for a particular bar code, and without having to put new stickers on every item.

Money

When you pay for your shopping, the payment will be handled by computer, as all banks use mainframe computers to keep track of accounts. Even if you spend cash it may have come from a dispenser, connected to the bank's main computer. These have details of all accounts, and may refuse to give you cash if you do not have enough money!

With a debit card, you can pay for shopping electronically. These plastic cards each have a unique number magnetically encoded on a stripe on the back. A card "reader" at the cash register is connected by special phone line to a main banking computer. When your card is put through the machine, it reads the card's number and tells the bank computer to transfer the amount you have spent from your account to the shop's.

This transfer is instant, and is called "electronic funds transfer", or EFT. The main bank computer contacts the computers of your bank and the shop's bank and tells them to transfer the money.

Cash dispenser

Printed material

Many books (like this one), magazines and newspapers are produced on computer systems. The text is written on a word processor and then fed into a computer running desktop publishing (DTP) software*. The designers then use the computer to make up pages - putting the type into different typefaces, adding headlines, coloured panels, page numbers and even scanning in photographs and other illustrations.

*For more on DTP (desktop publishing) systems, see page 21.

Computers in design and art

Computer graphics can be seen every day in films, television and computer games. They are not only used for entertainments, but also in business for training and marketing, for electronic information systems, and for simulators such as those used to train pilots.

Most microcomputers can run special graphics software packages and be used to produce pictures. Some dedicated computers have been developed just to produce graphics. However, the computer is just a tool: it is the artist or designer who provides the creativity and skill.

Computer art

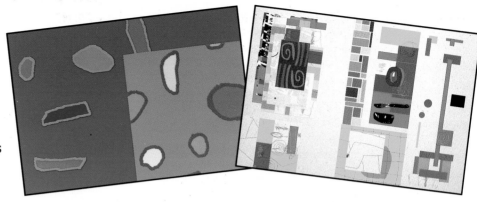

Most computer graphics are used commercially. However, fine artists are also exploring the exciting options that computers can offer

them. Here are some computer pictures by James Faure Walker who is Tutor in Computer Graphics at the Royal College of Art, London.

In-betweening

Kite   Bird

A computer can be programmed to turn one shape or picture into another one. It works out all the steps between the two pictures. This is known as "in-betweening" and is used in film animation.

Business graphics

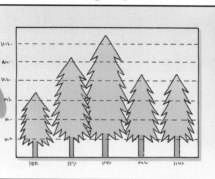

Good graphics can help to present information in a more easily understood and interesting way. Computers are used to display figures as charts and graphs for business presentations.

Games graphics

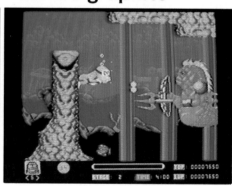

Computer and video games need fast-moving screens of graphics to go with the games. These pictures are usually programmed in low-level machine language, rather than using specialist graphics software.

Type design

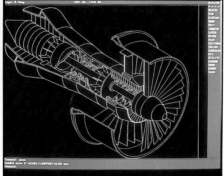

Letters are drawn up very big.

Many new typefaces are actually designed using a computer to draw up the letters. Computers make it easier to scale the letters down to different sizes to see what they look like, and if they are readable.

CAD-CAM

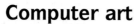

CAD stands for computer-aided design, CAM for computer-aided manufacture. CAD-CAM software is used in the design and manufacture of things, from buildings and bridges, to packaging and cars.

Computer landscapes

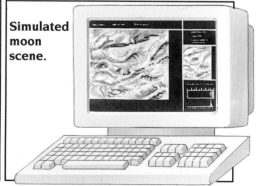

Simulated moon scene.

This picture of the Moon's surface was drawn by a computer using measurements taken by space probes. You can use the computer to "fly" over the realistic-looking landscape and see it from all angles.

TV graphics

The spectacular computer graphics effects that you can see on TV are created on dedicated TV graphics computers like the one below. Designers use them to create pictures from scratch and to manipulate images "grabbed" from video or film. Colours can be changed, images mixed together, effects added and pictures squeezed, squashed, tilted and even wrapped into different shapes, such as cylinders and spheres.

Instructions allow designers to choose styles such as pencil, airbrush, watercolour and so on.

Designers can use over a thousand colours.

The "pen" is used to draw on the sensitive graphics pad which transmits information to the screen.

Computerized buildings

Architects use computers and special software to help them design buildings and draw up building plans. Some programs can also show what a finished building will look like, inside and out. The computer can rotate the picture and show it from any different angle, as it has all the data for each view in memory. This is often called a "walk through", because the computer shows the scene as if you are actually walking round the building.

How pictures are displayed on screen

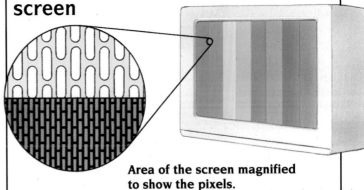

Area of the screen magnified to show the pixels.

The screen is divided into tiny squares called "pixels" (picture elements) which are turned on or off to make the pictures. Each pixel is controlled by a small portion of the computer's RAM. Using the graphics software, you give the computer information about the picture, telling it what pixels to turn on and in which colours.

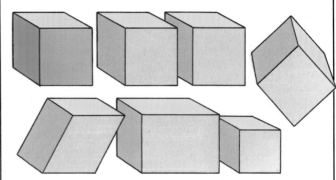

The information for the picture is stored in binary code and so it is very easy to alter. For instance you can change all the red areas to blue, instantly, and then change them back again if you do not like it. Pictures can be repeated, rotated, slanted, stretched, flipped over, made larger or smaller, filled with colour or patterns and moved round the screen.

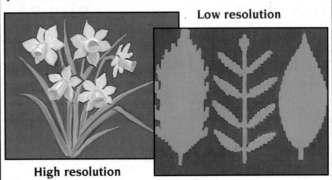

Low resolution

High resolution

The realism and detail of the picture depends upon how many pixels there are on the screen and how much memory the computer has for each one. This is called its "resolution". High resolution pictures like the one on the left are made up of many, small pixels. Low resolution pictures like the one on the right have fewer, chunky-looking pixels and use fewer colours.

Computer models

Sometimes it is easier to solve a problem, or test an idea, if you make a model of it. Computers are very good at this. For instance, if you give the computer details about an airport, it can put together all the information and provide a description or "model" of the airport and how it works. This model is presented as words, graphs, charts and pictures, not as a solid 3D model.

You can then change some of the information and the computer shows you what effect this will have. Computer models like this are called computer simulations.

Greenhouse simulator

Commercial gardeners use simulations to find out the best, and cheapest, conditions for growing crops and flowers. The computer is given information about the greenhouse and plants and then is programmed to work out the effects of changing the temperature, giving more or less water and other variables. As plants grow slowly it would take too long to try all these greenhouse conditions in real life. The computer can do it quickly, trying different variables to find the best combination.

Flight simulator

Computer simulations are very useful as they can save humans having to risk danger when learning a skill. Pilots, for example, learn to fly planes without even taking off, by using flight simulators like the one shown here. With a flight simulator, pilots can get used to flying the plane in complete safety, and without using any expensive fuel.

The simulator moves in three directions: yaw, pitch and roll.

Yaw

Roll

Pitch

The simulator is mounted on a platform which can move in three directions, just like a real plane. This motion is vital to make it feel real to the pilot inside.

The pilot sits in an exact replica of a real aircraft cockpit, with all the same controls and equipment.

Pneumatic legs move the simulator in a realistic way.

What the pilot sees

The windscreen is surrounded by a huge screen, on to which is projected a computer-generated landscape. This shows the runway as it would appear on landing and take-off, like the picture to the left. The computer also moves the simulator and changes the projected image in response to the pilot's use of the controls in the cockpit.

Traffic modelling

Controlling traffic flow in a large, busy city is a very complicated process. Computer modelling helps planners to do this efficiently. They can make a computer model of all the main roads, feed in data on the numbers of vehicles at different times and then experiment with variables.

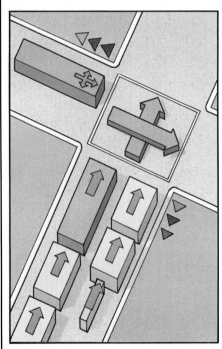

For example, by changing the positions, numbers and timing of traffic lights, re-routing trucks or making bus-only lanes, the computer can show traffic planners what effect this will have on car journey times.

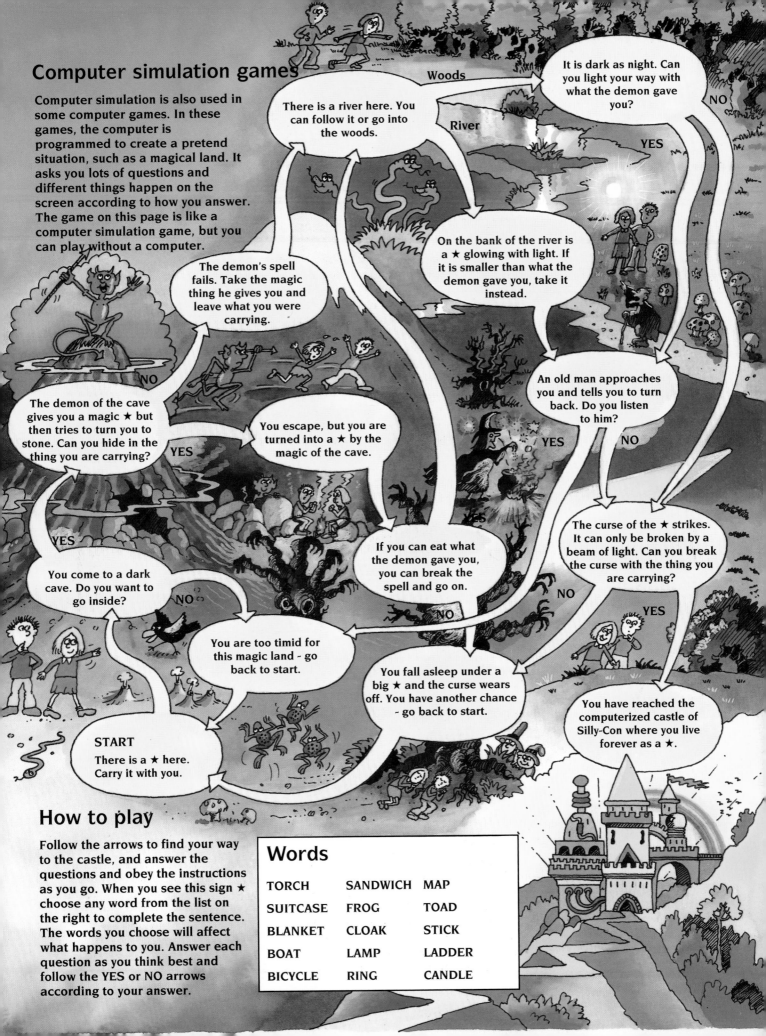

Computer simulation games

Computer simulation is also used in some computer games. In these games, the computer is programmed to create a pretend situation, such as a magical land. It asks you lots of questions and different things happen on the screen according to how you answer. The game on this page is like a computer simulation game, but you can play without a computer.

It is dark as night. Can you light your way with what the demon gave you?

There is a river here. You can follow it or go into the woods.

Woods

River

NO

YES

The demon's spell fails. Take the magic thing he gives you and leave what you were carrying.

On the bank of the river is a ★ glowing with light. If it is smaller than what the demon gave you, take it instead.

The demon of the cave gives you a magic ★ but then tries to turn you to stone. Can you hide in the thing you are carrying?

NO

You escape, but you are turned into a ★ by the magic of the cave.

An old man approaches you and tells you to turn back. Do you listen to him?

YES

YES

NO

YES

The curse of the ★ strikes. It can only be broken by a beam of light. Can you break the curse with the thing you are carrying?

You come to a dark cave. Do you want to go inside?

If you can eat what the demon gave you, you can break the spell and go on.

YES

NO

NO

NO

You are too timid for this magic land - go back to start.

You fall asleep under a big ★ and the curse wears off. You have another chance - go back to start.

YES

You have reached the computerized castle of Silly-Con where you live forever as a ★.

START
There is a ★ here. Carry it with you.

How to play

Follow the arrows to find your way to the castle, and answer the questions and obey the instructions as you go. When you see this sign ★ choose any word from the list on the right to complete the sentence. The words you choose will affect what happens to you. Answer each question as you think best and follow the YES or NO arrows according to your answer.

Words

TORCH	SANDWICH	MAP
SUITCASE	FROG	TOAD
BLANKET	CLOAK	STICK
BOAT	LAMP	LADDER
BICYCLE	RING	CANDLE

Computer firsts

The development of computers can be divided into three main stages, known as generations. The first generation was the large mainframes built with valves. The smaller, more reliable, computers built with transistors are called the second generation, and modern computers made with silicon chips are the third generation. Here are some of the main dates in the early history of computers.

1945 ENIAC, the first all-electronic machine, was built. It was more like a calculator than a present-day computer, though, as it could not store data or programs. ENIAC stands for Electronic Numerical Integrator and Calculator.

Manchester University Mark I

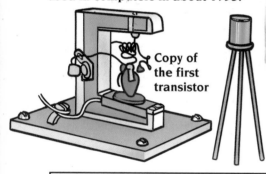

ENIAC

1947 A new kind of electronic component, called the transistor, was invented. Transistors were first used in computers in about 1953.

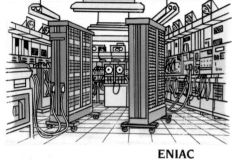

Copy of the first transistor

1948 The Manchester University Mark I, the first real computer (that is, one which could store a program of instructions) ran for 52 minutes on June 21.

Ferranti Mark I

1950 The Ferranti Mark I, based on the Manchester Mark I, was sold commercially in Europe.

1958 The first working integrated circuit was developed.

1960 The first "chips" - integrated circuits on chips of silicon - were produced.

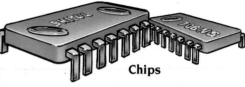

Chips

1964 The first computers built with integrated circuits were produced for the general market.

1975/6 The first small home computer, the Altair, was sold.

Sharp PC1211

1980 The first pocket computer, the Japanese Sharp PC1211, was produced.

1981 IBM introduced their small but powerful desktop micro, the PC (Personal Computer). Other manufacturers produced cheaper PC "clones" (computers with the same operating system and design as the IBM PC). PCs are the most widely used computers in the world.

First modern computer?

This machine, called the Analytical Engine, might have been the first modern computer. It was invented by an English mathematician, Charles Babbage, who lived from 1791 to 1871.

Babbage designed the machine to do complex sums and store the results at each stage in the calculations. It used a mechanical system, based on racks, levers and gears, but his ideas form the basis for the design of modern computers. However, the Analytical Engine was never built. Nor were any of the other, similar mechanical calculating machines which Babbage designed.

It is thought that Babbage's engines were not built due to lack of money and because at the time it was not possible to engineer them accurately enough. Eventually, though, one of these machines was actually built. The Difference Engine No.2 was constructed at the Science Museum in London, to celebrate the 200th anniversary of Babbage's birth in June 1991, and to test his designs. The Difference Engine worked, just as Babbage expected, and proved that his ideas were sound. It is a vast machine, consisting of 4,000 parts, weighing about 3 tonnes (tons) and standing 3.3m (11ft) long and 2.1m (7ft) tall.

Computer words

Here is a list of computer words and their meanings. If you want to know more about one of the words, look it up in the index, then turn to the pages for that word.

APPLICATION SOFTWARE Programs that make the computer perform a particular job, such as word processing.

BACK-UP STORE Information stored by computer on magnetic disks, tapes etc.

BINARY A number system based on two digits: "1" and "0".

BIT A binary digit, that is "1" or "0".

BUG An error in a computer program.

BYTE A group of eight binary digits which represents one unit of data in the computer's memory.

COMPUTER A machine that can accept data, process it according to a stored program of instructions and then output the results.

CPU (CENTRAL PROCESSING UNIT) The control centre of the computer which organizes all the other parts inside the computer.

DATA The information given to the computer for processing.

DATABASE A program that stores information on magnetic disks or tapes, in such a way that it can be accessed very quickly.

DISK A magnetic store for computer information.

DTP (DESKTOP PUBLISHING) Computer equipment and software used to produce printed matter, such as brochures and books.

FLOWCHART A chart showing the sequence of steps needed for a computer program.

HARDWARE All the computer equipment, including the computer itself, input, output and storage devices.

INPUT The data going into the computer and the process of putting it in.

KILOBYTE Often called "K", this is a measure of data storage and is 1,024 bytes.

MEGABYTE A measure of data storage, larger than K. It is over a million (1,024 x 1,024) bytes.

MEMORY The chips in the computer where information and instructions are stored in binary code.

MICROPROCESSOR A chip which can do the same jobs as the main parts of a computer.

MODEM A device which enables computers to communicate with each other, using telephone lines.

MOUSE An input device which you roll around on a desk to move an on-screen pointer to input commands. These commands are often icons (pictures).

OUTPUT The results of a computer's processing.

PRINTER A device which can print out words and/or pictures from a computer.

PROGRAM A set of instructions which tells the computer what to do.

PROGRAMMING LANGUAGE A computer language, such as BASIC, used to write programs that run on computers.

RAM (RANDOM ACCESS MEMORY) The part of the computer's memory where data, instructions and results are stored temporarily.

ROM (READ ONLY MEMORY) The part of the computer's memory containing a permanent store of instructions for the computer.

SOFTWARE Computer programs on disk or tape.

SYSTEM SOFTWARE Programs that control the basic workings of a computer.

VIRUS A bug deliberately, but secretly, introduced to a computer or software to cause problems for the user.

VDU (VISUAL DISPLAY UNIT) A TV-like screen on which information from the computer can be displayed. (Sometimes also known as a monitor.)

The future

This picture shows how dramatically computers have developed over the last 50 years, becoming ever smaller, cheaper and more powerful. The first computers could do relatively few calculations a second whereas a modern microcomputer can carry out millions of instructions each second.

If cars had developed at the same rate as computers, we would now be able to travel at thousands of kilometres (miles) per hour in a tiny, but powerful, personal vehicle which would use hardly any fuel, have many extra features and be a fraction of the price of existing cars.

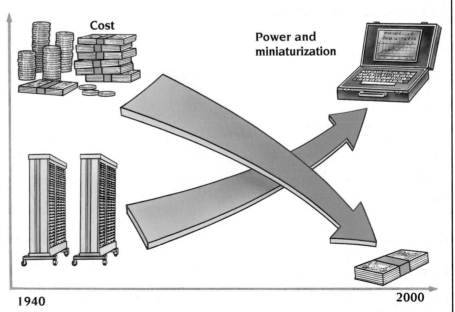

Cost

Power and miniaturization

1940

2000

Index

The publishers would like to thank the following people and organizations for their kind permission to use the photographs on the pages indicated.
Quantel (UK) Ltd: page 27
Alias Research Ltd: page 27

Answer to quiz on page 9
The word written in binary code is ROBOT

This edition first published in 1992 by Usborne Publishing Ltd., Usborne House, 83-85 Saffron Hill, London EC1N 8RT, England.

The name Usborne and the device ♛ are Trade Marks of Usborne Publishing Ltd.

Printed in Portugal.

©1981, 1992 Usborne Publishing Ltd. Based on material first published in 1981 as the Usborne Guide to Computers. All rights reserved. No part of this publication may be reproduced, stored in a retrieval system or transmitted in any form or by any means, electronic, mechanical, photocopying, recording, or otherwise, without the prior permission of the publisher.